A Giant First-Start Reader

This easy reader contains only 37 different words, repeated often to help the young reader develop word recognition and interest in reading.

Basic word list for *Fun in the Snow*

a	falls	round
along	fort	snow
and	go	snowman
at	in	soft
bright	is	the
build	it	then
can	like	to
cold	look	today
come	made	up
day	night	we
deep	of	white
do	play	you
down		

Fun in the Snow

Written by Laura Damon

Illustrated by Diane Paterson

Troll Associates

Library of Congress Cataloging in Publication Data

Damon, Laura.
  Fun in the snow.

    Summary: Two young bears are delighted to see that
deep white snow has come down during the night, because
now they can go out and play in it.
    [1. Snow—Fiction. 2. Bears—Fiction. 3. Stories
in rhyme] I. Paterson, Diane, 1946-   ill.
II. Title.
PZ8.3.D184Fu   1988   [E]   87-10843
ISBN 0-8167-1081-3 (lib. bdg.)
ISBN 0-8167-1082-1 (pbk.)

Look at the snow . . .
soft and white.

Down it falls,
deep in the night.

Look at the snow . . .
deep and white.

Look at the snow . . .
cold and bright.

Today we can play.

We can play in the snow.

Up, up, up . . .

and down we go!

Round . . . round . . .

and round we go!

Today we can build.

We can build in the snow.

We can build a fort—
a fort made of snow!

We can build a snowman—
a snowman made of snow!

Today we can go.
We can go in the snow.

We can go up.

We can go down.

We can go round and round and round.

Look at the snow . . .
deep and white.

Look at the snow . . .
cold and bright.

Do you like the snow?

Do you like to play?

Then come along—
today is the day!